TALES FROM
WRESCAL LANE

By
MICK FOLEY

with illustrations by
JILL THOMPSON

POCKET BOOKS

World
Wrestling
Entertainment

New York   London   Toronto   Sydney

To my two littlest wrescals,
Mickles and Hughie

DudLeys Do RiGHT

The night was still on Wrescal Lane;
no child or bird was peeping.
But little Steph just tossed and turned—
for her there was no sleeping.

For tiny Steph had her heart set on
a doll called Honey Bunny.
But she could not buy the cuddly toy,
because she had no money.

"I need to find a way," she thought,
"to earn a couple dollars."
She knew she could not ask her dad,
for all he'd do was holler.

For hours young Steph tried to think,
but all to no avail!
Then she had a great idea:
"I'll have a small yard sale!"

When morning came, she went upstairs and opened up a trunk.
"I think that I can sell," she hoped, "some of Daddy's junk."

She asked her brother Shane for help, but little Shane got mad.
"You will be in trouble, Steph, once I **TELL MY DAD!**"

But little Steph just smiled so cute and dragged the box downstairs.
She put her dad's stuff out on the lawn on a table with two chairs.

First one neighbor came to look, but in an hour there were many.
Lita, Matt, The Rock, and Kane, each one had brought their pennies.

The children looked and bought some things and played well with one another.
Then Lita frowned and said to Matt, "Here come the Dudley Brothers!"

The Dudley Boys both seemed to love finding ways of starting trouble.
One Dudley Boy was bad enough, but together they were double!

D-Von laughed and said to Steph, "Neither me nor Bubba Ray
would pay a single penny for your father's old toupee!"

Bubba sneered at Steph and said,
"Do you think I am a kook?
Who else would buy this helmet
that was once worn by Faarooq?"

Shane got up and yelled quite loud; he'd become an angry lad.
"Pay up for that helmet now—or else I'll **TELL MY DAD!**"

The Dudley Boys just laughed out loud, and to prove that they were able, both picked up young helpless Shane and **SLAMMED** him through the table.

The yard sale stuff
flew everywhere
from Stamford to Hoboken.
When it landed in the grass,
ALL OF iT
WAS BROKEN!

A title belt was smashed to bits!

The toupee, it was torn.

The helmet, it lay damaged too,
the one Faarooq had worn.

It was a perfect day on Wrescal Lane; the skies were blue and sunny.
But for Stephanie, the day was gray. She cried, "I'll never get my Bunny!"

The tears then fell from Steph's blue eyes. She'd never felt this sad.
Shane just lay on the ground and groaned, "I'm gonna **TELL MY DAD.**"

The Dudley Boys, they laughed and laughed. To them this scene was funny.
D-Von yelled, "I don't care if you ever get your Bunny!"

When Bubba laughed, his belly shook, for it was round and lardy.
"Today's our birthday," he proclaimed. "Who's coming to our party?"

Now no one really liked the boys. No one wanted to be near them.
But all the children acted nice because everybody feared them!

The Rock and Kane first raised their hands.
Then, Lita and Matt Hardy.

Even Shane and Stephanie replied
that they'd come over to the party.

As evening fell on Wrescal Lane, the little ones were headed
to the last house on the left, the one everybody dreaded.

None of them had empty hands; they carried gifts or toys.
No one wanted to be slammed by angry Dudley Boys.

The Dudley Boys grabbed for the gifts as fast as they were able.
They scooped up all the presents and placed them on a table.

There were no games or music played, no visits from a clown.
Birthdays should bring lots of smiles. All this one brought was frowns.

A big birthday cake was brought outside,
        almost too great to handle.
Bubba looked at Kane and said,
        "Wanna help blow out
        the candles?"

The kindness seemed a little strange,
but Kane gave in to Bubba's wish.
Then D-Von snuck up from behind
and threw his head down with a

SQUISH!

The Dudley Boys laughed at Kane and said, "Stay in your places."
Then even though the cake was squashed, the boys stuffed it down their faces!

When the two were full, Bubba said,
        "I'm tired of being pleasant.
    Now all you babies gather 'round
            while we open up our presents!"

They opened up their gift from The Rock,
who'd emptied out his bank
to buy the Dudleys matching glasses,
but neither one said thanks.

D-Von glared at present two,
to both the boys from Shane.
He said, "You better hope we like it,
or else you'll feel some pain!"

When unwrapped, they saw two gifts
and each one looked the same:
a painted picture of both boys,
each in a matching frame.

D-Von grumbled, "Hmm, not bad...
I expected something badder."
Matt and Lita knew their gift was next,
so they looked down from their ladder.

Matt and Lita, both were small—
neither wanted to get hurt.
So they'd both spent all their money
and bought each boy a shirt.

The shirts were blue with red pinstripes and said, "The Dudleys Rule."
Both kids held their breath in fear until D-Von said, "That's cool."

"Kane, you're next, and you'd better hope we like it," Bubba grumbled.
But cake had gotten in Kane's eyes, and it caused the boy to stumble.

Poor Kane, he could not help himself—he fell into the ladder!

Which tipped and fell with frightening force
and caused the birthday gifts to

The picture frames were crushed to bits and both pairs of glasses broken.
A piece of glass was later found on the south side of Hoboken.

The shirts the Dudleys thought were cool flew right before their eyes,
and landed where the Dudleys' dog had left a small surprise.

The Dudleys both looked awful sad,
of that there's no denying.
Then their eyes filled up with tears,
and both boys started crying.

The other kids began to laugh.
They thought it was a riot.
All except young, sweet Steph,
who managed to stay quiet.

She walked up to the crying boys,
who by now were thrashing wildly.
They seemed to be a little sad,
and that's to put it mildly.

She patted D-Von's crying head
and patted Bubba's hand.
She said, "I hope that both you boys
will finally understand

"That being mean and bad and rude
is not a bit of fun.
You've made the other children sad
with the mean things that you've done.

"So dry your eyes when we go home,
and rethink your naughty deeds.
And realize one day these kids you scare
might be the friends you'll need."

The party guests then left the yard.
They went home and off to bed.
And Stephanie, she fell asleep
with thoughts of Dudleys in her head.

When morning came, she arose,
not to the chirping of a bird.
It wasn't little tweet-tweet-tweets,
but someone knocking that she heard.

She went downstairs and threw back the door
to greet the newborn day.
But standing right in front of her
were D-Von and Bubba Ray!

Their little eyes were red and sore
because they'd cried all night.
Were they going to cry again?
Steph really thought they might.

Instead they held out a little box,
and D-Von said, "We thought you
might forgive us for the things we've done
if you like the gift we brought you."

The moment that Steph saw the gift
her day turned bright and sunny!

"THANK YOU!
THANK YOU,
DUDLEY
BOYS!

YOU BROUGHT ME
HONEY BUNNY!"

These days the Dudleys still play rough, but they never are a pain
to Steph or Shane or all the kids who live on Wrescal Lane.

KURT'S COASTER CRISIS

The sun shone down on Wrescal Lane;
the sky was clear and blue.
"It's a great day for some rides," said Kurt,
"and that, my friends, is true."

The children stepped inside Kurt's house,
but before they left to play,
Kurt cooked a hearty breakfast—
a great way to start the day.

He scrambled eggs for Triple H; Mick and Stacy asked for toast.
While they waited for the bread to brown, Kurt began to boast.

The children were all used to this,
for Kurt was quite a boaster.
"I bet I'll be the only one
to ride the roller coaster."

Kurt then laughed and reminded them
about the trip they'd planned.
"This is not a kiddie park—
no, we're going to Vinnieland!"

Vinnieland was a new theme park
built by Vince McMahon.
And its Titan roller coaster
was the tallest in the land.

"It's true! It's true!" Kurt reconfirmed,
as he took toast from the toaster.
"I will be the only kid
to ride the roller coaster."

When the food was eaten, Kurt stood and said, "Let's go!"
"Just a minute," Stacy said. "We're waiting for Al Snow."

Kurt looked out and saw young Al, who struggled with his bike.
"I can't believe you invited him, the one wrescal I don't like."

Mick then pleaded, "Let him come," as Al fumbled with the pedals. "All right, all right!" Kurt gave in. "But don't let him touch my medals."

The medals were Kurt's pride and joy—he'd never been the same since coming home with triple gold from the World Wide Wrescal Games.

He once had been a humble child,
but after he won gold,
His friends had grown a wee bit tired
of the stories that he told.

Nonetheless, Kurt was their friend,
so they tried to understand.
They wouldn't let his bragging
spoil a day at Vinnieland.

So off the children headed,
without further hesitation,
and caught the next departing train
at the Wrescal Lane Train Station.

Kurt sat down inside the train and eyed his medals with great pride.
He knew he'd be a champ again—aboard the coaster ride.

Then Hunter yawned. "We're sleepy, Kurt, you're being such a pain.
You have flapped your jaws nonstop since we left Wrescal Lane."

"Fine!" yelled Kurt. "Go to sleep. You'll miss out on all my glory."
Then a tiny voice was heard saying, "I'd like to hear a story."

Kurt looked down at little Al, who sat with his toy head.
       "So you'd like to hear a story? I've got another plan instead!

"Shut your mouth. Don't talk to me. That is my demand.
          Pretend you do not know me when we get to Vinnieland!"

               The train chugged on toward the park,
                      and while their friends were sleeping . . .
                   Kurt smugly smiled when he heard small sobs—
                          little Al was weeping.

The silver train screeched to a stop. The children sprang awake.
Stacy saw the castle, in the distance by the lake.

The children simply stood in awe, for truly it was grand.
A place where children's dreams come true—a place called Vinnieland.

Kurt stared down at his gold and, without the slightest hinting,
started running at full speed—for the entrance he was sprinting.

All the children bolted too, and joined Kurt in the race.
All, that is, except poor Al, who could not keep up the pace.

The struggling boy made Mick sad,
for the two of them were pals.
Then, as he had done for many years,
Mick picked up and carried Al.

His face turned red to match his shirt,
but he made it to the end.
Al hopped down and gave Mick a hug.
He said, "You are my best friend."

"That's enough," said Triple H.
"Cut out the sappy stuff!
We're going to the coaster now—
it could get a little rough!"

"Too rough for Al!" Kurt yelled out,
but Stacy said, " Be quiet."
Al looked up and seemed quite scared,
saying, "I guess that I could try it."

Mick then said, "I've got a plan
that makes a lot of sense—
a way for Al to have some fun,
in case the coaster's too intense.

"Let's all go on a small ride first,
and if Al's a little frightened,
Then he can watch while we all ride
the roller coaster Titan."

The children walked, and made a left
at a Christmas shop called Scrooge's.
Up ahead a sign proclaimed,
"The Spookhouse of the Stooges."

The ride would be a perfect test,
the children all agreed.
The spookhouse cars squeaked a bit,
but they traveled at a slow speed.

Stacy rode with Triple H;
Mick doubled with Al Snow.
Kurt Angle rode all by himself
and was the first to go.

Upon their reemergence, the kiddies seemed quite pleased.
All of them but Al, that is, who had his heads between his knees.

A callous Kurt threw up his hands and said, "Hey, what the heck?
If there was an award for biggest baby, he'd have gold around his neck."

Stacy tried to dry Al's eyes, but his tears were uncontrollable.
Mick did his best to comfort him, but Al was inconsolable.

A giant voice then filled the air; it boomed, "What's the matter, son?
Were you scared a bit by Brisco's dress, or the ghost of Patterson?"

The voice belonged to Vince McMahon, who seemed to understand.
He wiped away all Al's tears and took him by the hand.

"Why not try some smaller rides, like Edge's Awesome Train?
You can ride with both my kids, Stephanie and Shane."

"Take the little wimp," sneered Kurt. "Our load needs to be lightened.
Now, if you have got the guts, let's leave and ride the Titan."

The Titan seemed to touch the stars.
Its cars dropped from the clouds.
The children seemed a little scared,
but Kurt Angle laughed out loud.

"Stacy, Mick, and Triple H...have
you three seen a ghost, or...
maybe you're not tough enough
to ride this roller coaster."

Stacy started shaking
as she climbed into the car.
Mick sure seemed to hesitate
as he pulled down his safety bar.

The coaster car went

CLICK,
CLICK,
CLICK

as it began its steep ascent.
Hunter thought about his guts—
like where the heck they went!

Suddenly, the car **PLUNGED** down!
It felt like they were **FLYING!**
Amidst familiar wrescal laughs,
Mick heard someone crying.

The Titan's track **ZIGGED** and **ZAGGED,**
and when it looped the loop,
Stacy looked at Triple H and said,
"I think I smell a poop!"

The wrescals savored every thrill,
but when the car screeched to a halt,
Kurt quickly jumped up from his seat
with a mighty vault.

For a moment they all thought that he
went back to ride that coaster
or stopped to have a tasty snack
at Stone Cold's Country Roasters.

Instead, they saw him run on past
a ride called Heat and Pushes.
He zipped to the left at J.R.'s Steaks
and disappeared into the bushes.

The children searched throughout the park until their feet were throbbing.
Then from behind a massive oak, they heard Kurt Angle sobbing!

"It's just one ride," Stacey coaxed. "Kurt, your day, it isn't spoiled."
"It is, too! It's true, it's true. My wrestling singlet's soiled!"

The wrescals tried hard not to laugh when they saw the singlet sagging.
For Kurt had really been a jerk—mean and always bragging.

Instead they tried to help their friend, whom they liked despite his ego.
"I promise not to boast," Kurt vowed, "on trips wherever we go."

His helpful friends searched for new clothes, but all to no avail,
till a small sign on Jabroni Drive read, "Wrestling Singlet Sale."

When Kurt tried on his new outfit, his chest swelled up with pride.
"Maybe we should all find Al," he said, "and go on some smaller rides."

For hours, the five friends
laughed and played
on Edge's Awesome Train.
And Kurt let Al Snow wear his gold,
all the way to Wrescal Lane.

Mick Foley's proceeds will be used
to build an early childhood education center
in the Philippines.